surf
1978

For my papa –
the eternal source of
joy and happiness

For my mama – the
eternal source of
love and wisdom

First published 2019 by Two Hoots
This edition published 2020 by Two Hoots
an imprint of Pan Macmillan
The Smithson, 6 Briset Street,
London, EC1M 5NR
Associated companies throughout the world
www.panmacmillan.com
ISBN 978-1-5098-8227-4
Text and illustrations copyright © Elina Ellis 2019
Moral rights asserted.

1 3 5 7 9 8 6 4 2
A CIP catalogue record for this book is available from the British Library.
Printed in China
The illustrations in this book were created using
pen, ink, gouache and Photoshop.

www.twohootsbooks.com

THE TRUTH ABOUT
OLD PEOPLE

Elina Ellis

TWO HOOTS

My grandparents are *really* old.

They have wrinkly faces,
a little bit of hair, and funny teeth.

I've been hearing lots of strange
things about old people.

Some people say old people are

NOT MUCH FUN.

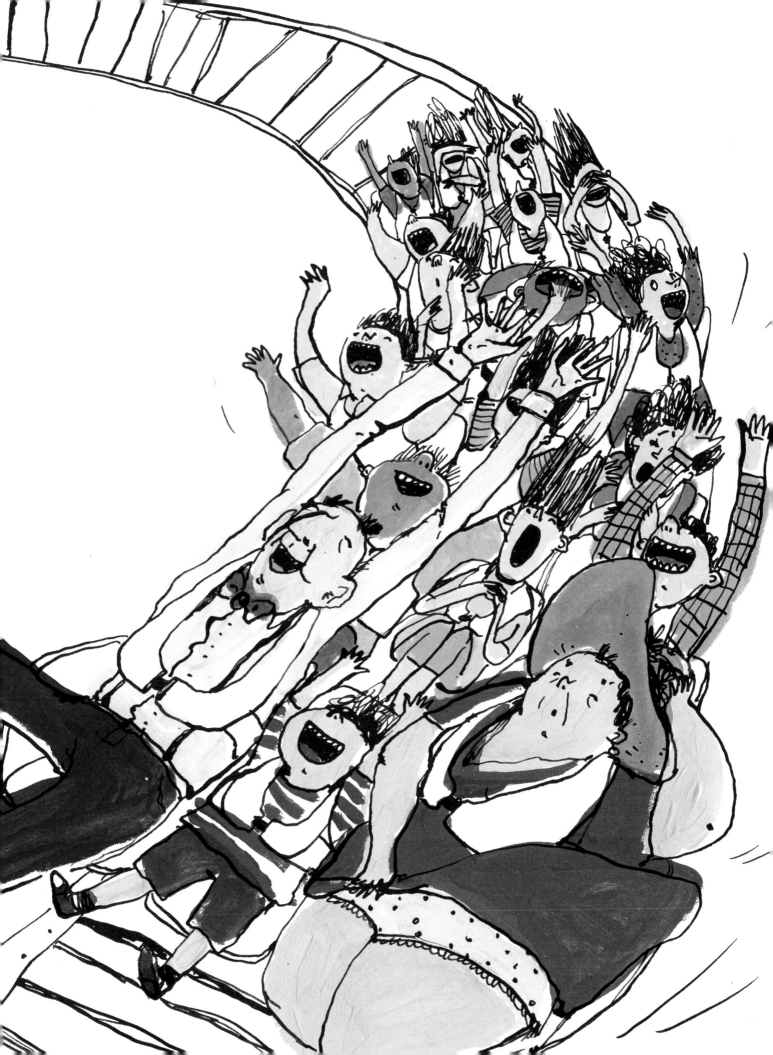

They say that old people are

old people are

and old people are

NOT BENDY.

Someone told me old people are

SCARED

of new things,

OLD

PEOPLE

DON'T

DANCE,

and old people
definitely don't care for
ROMANCE.

They say that old people are

QUIET,

and old people are

NOT AT ALL
ADVENTUROUS.

But I know the
truth about old people.

Old people are . . .

ZING!

A note from the author

Older people are brilliant, don't you think?
When I was little I loved spending time with
my grandparents. I couldn't understand why
some people didn't want to get older.

I still don't understand. There is no "use by" date
on human beings! We mature, evolve, expand,
transform. We grow. Older people have more
to give, because they have learned so much during
their long life: more wisdom, more empathy,
more appreciation, more freedom of spirit,
more love, and in many cases more joy.

This book is a celebration of being happy
and full of life at any age.

ELINA ELLIS